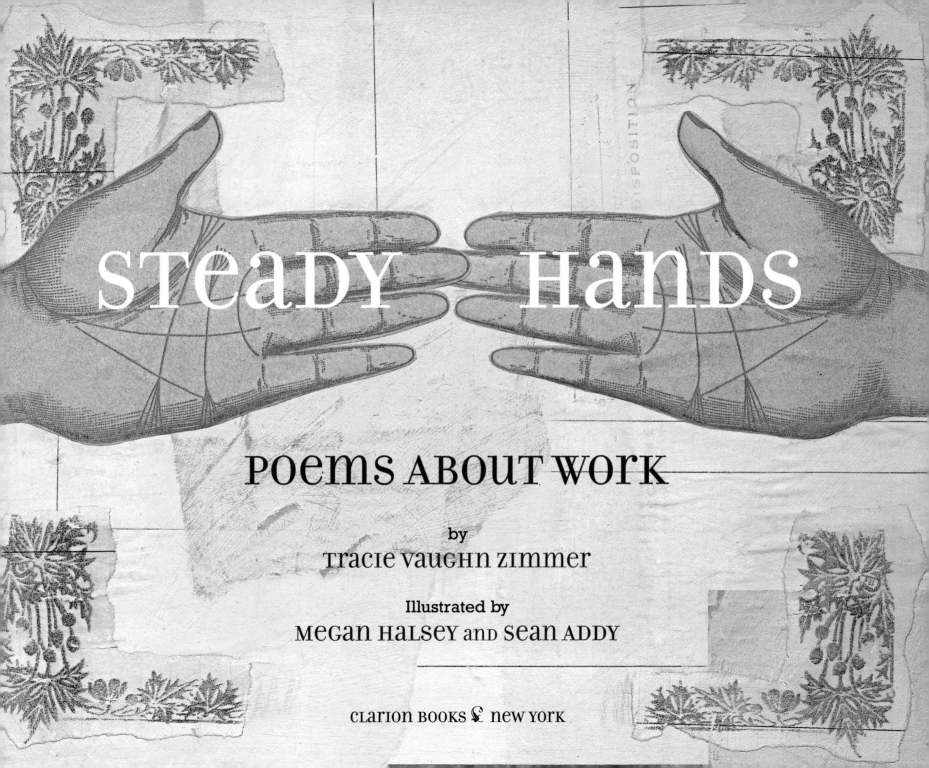

STEADY HANDS

POEMS ABOUT WORK

by
TRACIE VAUGHN ZIMMER

Illustrated by
MEGAN HALSEY AND SEAN ADDY

CLARION BOOKS ❧ NEW YORK

Clarion Books
an imprint of Houghton Mifflin Harcourt Publishing Company
215 Park Avenue South, New York, NY 10003
Text copyright © 2009 by Tracie Vaughn Zimmer
Illustrations copyright © 2009 by Megan Halsey and Sean Addy

The illustrations were executed in mixed media.
The text was set in 12-point Rockwell.

www.clarionbooks.com

Printed in Singapore

Library of Congress Cataloging-in-Publication Data

Zimmer, Tracie Vaughn.
Steady hands: poems about work / by Tracie Vaughn Zimmer ; illustrated by Megan Halsey and Sean Addy.
p. cm.
ISBN 978-0-618-90351-1
1. Children's poetry, American. 2. Occupations—Juvenile poetry. I. Halsey, Megan, ill. II. Addy, Sean, ill. III. Title.

PS3626.I489S74 2009
811'.6—dc22
2007038848

TWP 10 9 8 7 6 5 4 3 2 1

For my dad, Carl Vaughn,
and my brother, Paul Vaughn,
with love and gratitude
for all that your steady hands provide
—T.V.Z.

For my mother,
Nancy, and her loving hands
—M.H.

To Megan,
without your help,
I wouldn't have my "Steady Hands"!
—S.A.

contents

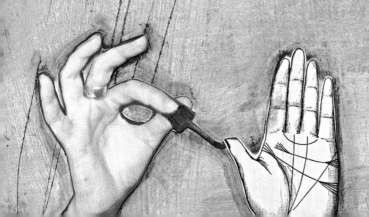

morning

Rooster nudges
the sun out of bed.

Alarms jangle,
sing, or speak
to restless dreamers.

Hot showers and fresh coffee
transform zombies
into humans,
while razors, combs,
toothpaste, and brushes
work in two-minute shifts.

Backpacks and briefcases
swallow books
and notes for breakfast.

Engines hum
heels click
and doors thud
behind ambitions.

7

8

FISHerman

Whistling, the fisherman
kneels in the prow
of his boat.
His thick, calloused hands
mend nets
untangle lines
then unlock a large tackle box
with compartments
full of bright lures—
a false candy store
for foolish fish
that opens before the sun
has stretched her arms
into morning.

Only tides and storms
supervise
the fisherman.

Baker

Snowy flour dusts the early
lavender light
in the backroom of the bakery.
With each
flap
roll
flap
the baker's hands
disappear
and reappear
in the folds
of dough.

flower market owner

For the next five months
the market owner
will arrive with daylight
to mulch the walkway
water the hanging ferns
set out flats of impatiens and petunias
deadhead begonias
and faded geraniums.

His shoes may be caked in mud,
his back and arms as stiff as oak branches,
but it's worth it
to spy finches snacking on
coneflower seeds
and hear cardinals declaring:
Spring!
Spring!
Spring!

Tow Truck Driver

The tow truck driver
fishes in the city:
a taxi
a sportscar
and a minivan—
three keepers
reeled in
before breakfast.

12

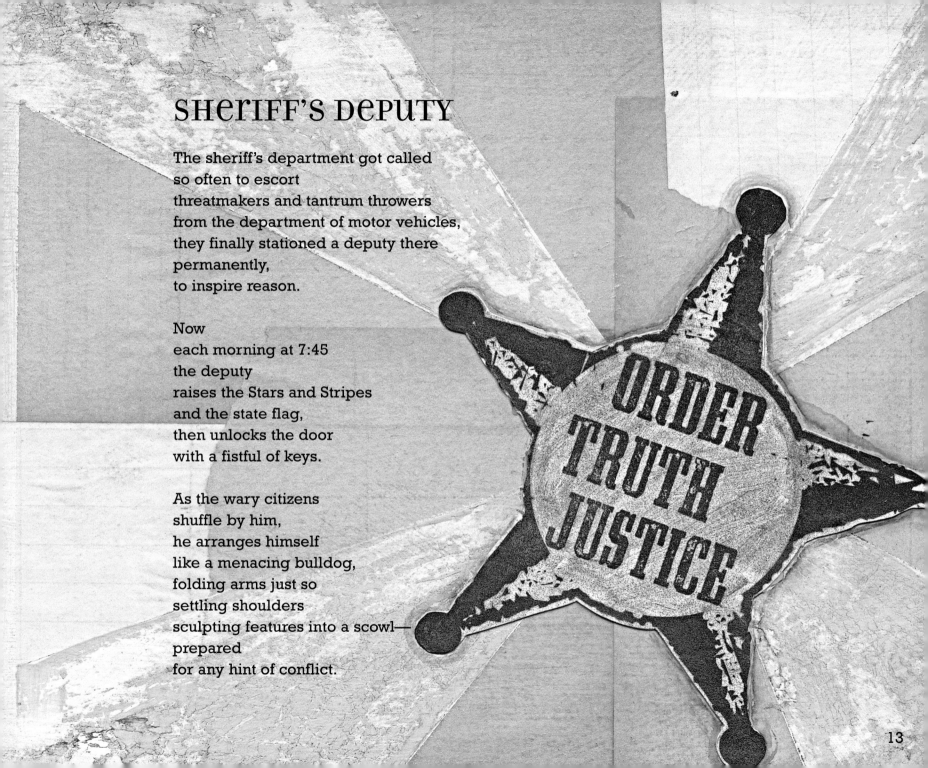

Sheriff's Deputy

The sheriff's department got called
so often to escort
threatmakers and tantrum throwers
from the department of motor vehicles,
they finally stationed a deputy there
permanently,
to inspire reason.

Now
each morning at 7:45
the deputy
raises the Stars and Stripes
and the state flag,
then unlocks the door
with a fistful of keys.

As the wary citizens
shuffle by him,
he arranges himself
like a menacing bulldog,
folding arms just so
settling shoulders
sculpting features into a scowl—
prepared
for any hint of conflict.

ORDER
TRUTH
JUSTICE

ELECTRICIAN

The electrician
hops out of her oversized pickup truck,
clips a heavy tool belt around
faded blue jeans,
puts on an orange hardhat,
raises a hand to the carpenters
already on the roof,
grabs a large thermos of coffee
and a dented cooler filled with lunch,
tucks rolled blueprints under one arm,
climbs the rugged path
to the unfinished house
in worn boots
stained dark
by dirt and clay,
then spends all day
unspooling
an electric web of wires.

welder

Like a knight preparing for battle,
the welder
pulls on his heavy gloves,
tips the helmet
over his eyes.

In an instant,
fireworks fountain
as mighty metal
drips in beads
guided by steady hands.

15

organizer

Her house was always orderly—
kids' toys sorted by category
canned goods lining pantry shelves
in alphabetical order.
She got to helping friends
organize their kitchens and closets,
and soon enough
she had a booming business.

She organized whole families,
turning their clutter and chaos
into order and routine,
so kids could find
instruments and gym clothes
tax receipts were filed
household maintenance performed.

When she was done,
families found time
to try new recipes
plan elaborate vacations
even play board games together.

16

And when one of her clients
moved away,
people fought over who would
get the open spot,
and she took applications
and interviewed
until a worthy family
was found.

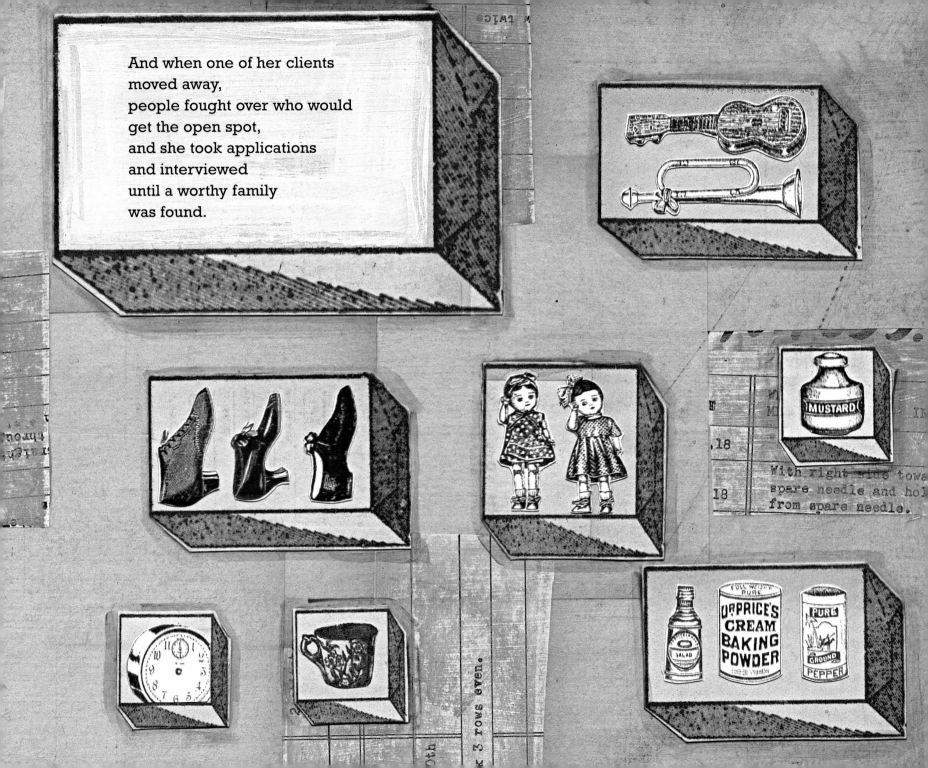

writer

Paid daydreamer
imaginary soothsayer
odd-fact researcher,
the writer
hovers like a hummingbird
by the
answering machine
computer
mailbox,
holding her breath while
scanning e-mails
listening to messages
sifting through junk mail
waiting, waiting,
forever waiting,
for the next
check
project
or call.

Artist

Curled up in the wide lap
of an overstuffed chair,
the artist
studies the eyes of a Picasso portrait
the hands of a Degas dancer
and the palette of a Pissarro landscape,
jumps up
begins ferreting through jars, bottles,
and boxes in her studio,
unearths
a skeleton key,
pearl buttons, a silver nut,
a pinch of lace,
and a stretch of copper wire.

Sketching
painting
cutting
gluing,
she assembles her vision
layer upon layer
until a small frog
leaps beneath her ribs
and she knows—
it's done.

cafeteria cook

The cafeteria cook
opens five jumbo cans each
of diced tomatoes,
yellow corn,
and tomato sauce
stirs them all
into the boiling chili
in a pot fashioned for giants.

As the raucous line
files past,
he gently reminds the children—
just as their parents would—
to choose some fruit
for dessert.

exterminator

When Bug-Bee-Gone's owner
hit the Powerball in the lotto,
he retired
to live—and fish every day—
on Lake Cumberland,
handing off the business
to his brother-in-law.

The new owner took some ribbing
down at the bowling alley
for battling bugs for a living.
The guys got to calling him Roach,
and the name stuck.

But he doesn't care,
not really.
He spends his days
ridding homes of
termites, carpenter ants,
even honeybees.
It may not be glamorous,
but it's steady—
with *some* critter
forever trying
to live rent-free!

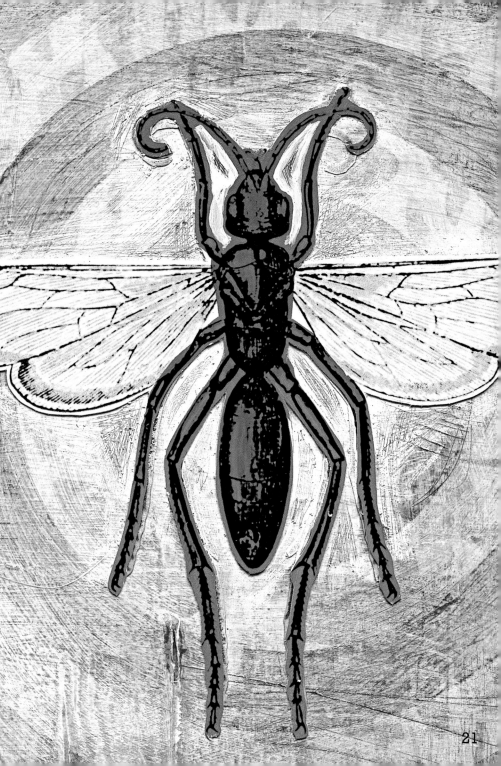

Retail Clerk

The clerk
is glad she doesn't have to see
what becomes of the clothes she sells—
the perfectly folded
pastel polo shirt
crumpled up
on a customer's bathroom floor,
the suede jacket with
hand-embroidered trim
marred by a messy lunch.

And now that she's signed
a lease
on a studio apartment
all
her
own,
never again will she have to witness
the mistreatment of
her discount discoveries—
like that salmon-colored silk scarf,
pilfered by her roommate
and discarded under the futon couch—
before she's even had the chance
to wear them
once!

miss Thomas

miss Harvey

mr. [illegible]

M. Simms

Job Applicants

personnel administrator

A secret:
the personnel administrator knows
ten minutes
into the interview
whether the applicant
will get the job—
or not.

Attire is judged
not for following fashion's trend
but for being spotless
professional
pressed.
Fingernails
don't lie,
and neither do shoes.

But it's the voice
that's the key:
sincere and enthusiastic—
or just calculating
payday.

LIFEGUARD

Lanky legs
slathered in sunscreen
nose covered by an army of freckles
heavy eyes
shielded by dark glasses,
the lifeguard
sits upright,
blows his whistle
at the dad

who cannonballed his son
into the deep end,
resumes slouched position
and his studied disinterest
in all the preteens
twittering below
his summer throne.

teacher

Everyone knows
the teacher's tasks:
creating bulletin-board displays
writing challenging tests
preparing perfect lessons
instructing, demonstrating, explaining.

But not everyone knows
the teacher's secret torments:
a lesson that knotted understanding
a bright kid who refuses to be inspired
flames of words thrown in frustration—

all heavier
to haul home
than the papers, projects, and lessons
bulging out of her bag.

surgeon

Green scrubs tied,
blue booties slipped over polished shoes,
clear plastic guard flipped down over
eyes that now need glasses
to read the medical chart,
the surgeon
never glances at the face
of the patient
behind the paper tent,
just studies the pale, puckered flesh
waiting to be parted
like overripe fruit.

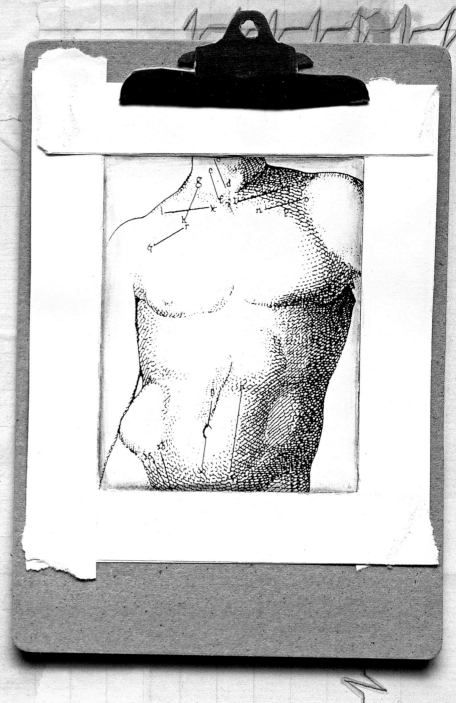

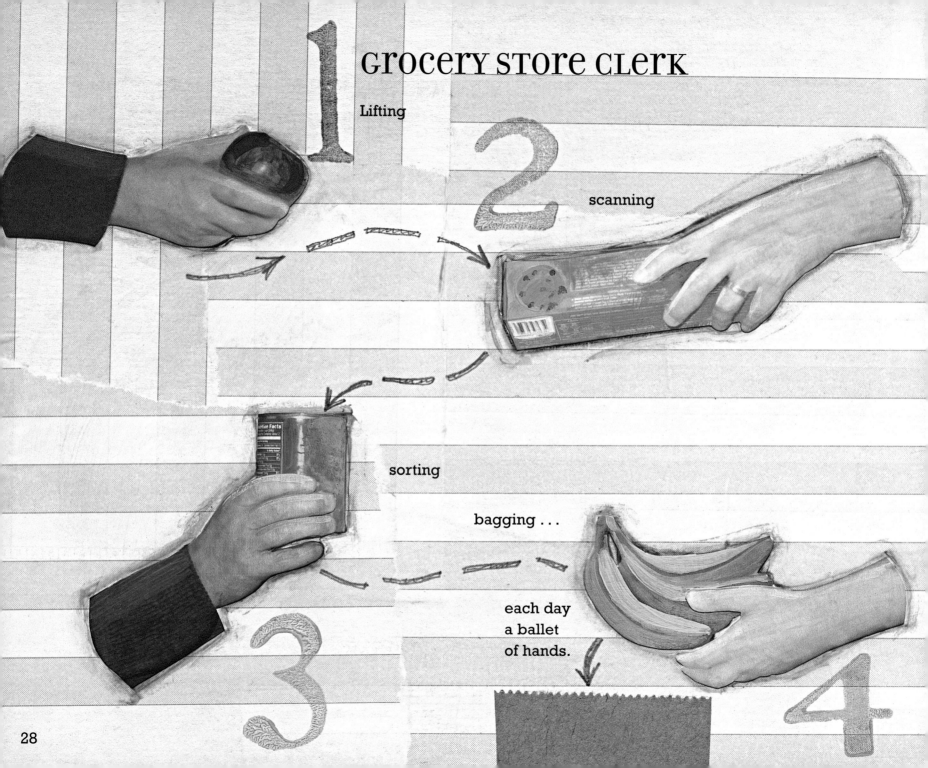

grocery store clerk

1 Lifting

2 scanning

sorting

bagging . . .

each day
a ballet
of hands.

3

4

Librarian

Logging onto his blog,
the librarian reviews
a graphic novel he scored
at a conference in Toronto.
He edits
a podcast interview
with a new voice
in the poetry slam scene,

adds friends to the teen library
Internet café.
Then he
grabs some sodas and
bags of snacks
and heads downstairs
to open the all-guy book club
that meets just after school.

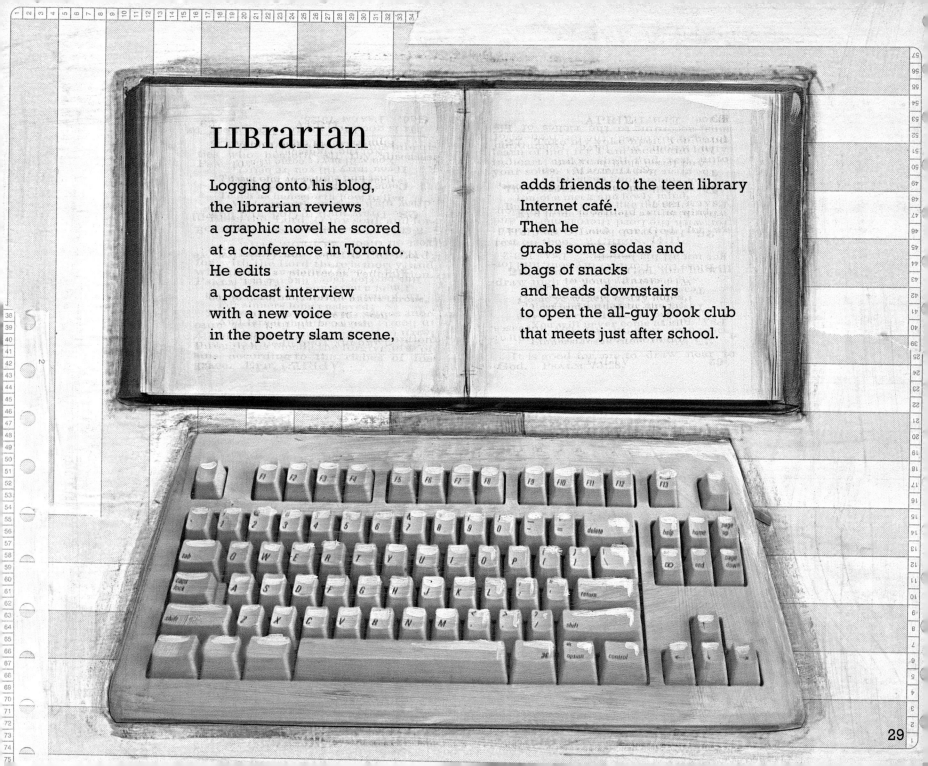

29

BALLET INSTRUCTOR

The four-year-olds
stand with right hands on the barre
tights wrinkled at the knees
slippered feet fidgeting
but faces turned
toward the instructor,
who poses,
chin tilted confidently
lips set in a soft smile
for her fresh charges
left arm arched
overhead
like the pale neck of a swan.

The music begins,
and she leads them
in their first steps
toward grace.

FLIGHT ATTENDANT

Most flights are monotonous:
polite business people
whiny toddlers
weary vacationers
so vulnerable looking
with their mouths half open,
heads tilted in sleep.

But serving
this odd concoction
of people
was his ticket
(free ticket anywhere)
out of a claustrophobic
town of two thousand
where, as a child,
he would stop
(even on his bicycle)
and dream
about the planes he saw
skimming through clouds.

31

DOG Walker

They say
the neighborhood dog walker
suffered a nervous breakdown,
walked away from a partnership
in a law firm downtown.

Truth was:
the predictable company of dogs
with their soulful eyes
and eager affection
didn't give him nightmares
or cold sweats
the way standing before
a glowering judge and jury did.

Besides,
a dog's mess
can be cleaned up.

park ranger

On Mondays
the park ranger
stays chained
to the information booth
answering the same
three questions
again and again:
9:00 P.M.
half a mile on the left
twelve and under.

But the rest of the week
she works the morning shift
clearing litter
sawing up fallen branches
hauling pine straw
to mark the trails—
and the only questions
come from migrating geese
asking each other
again and again
for directions home.

Information

bank teller

Fingers tapping
numbers and codes
like an old-fashioned Morse operator,
the bank teller watches
withdrawals
deposits
overdrafts
blink across the blue computer screen.

Double-checking the count
of crisp tens, twenties,
and hundred-dollar bills,
he slips them into white envelopes
for waiting customers
pops a mint
then studies the scrolling numbers
from Wall Street
on a monitor overhead.

administrative assistant

The administrative assistant
answers the phone
cheerfully,
files the folders
flawlessly,
enters new data
diligently,
types ten letters
speedily,

exits at five
precisely.

FLORIST

Arms crossed for warmth
in the walk-in refrigerator,
the florist
studies the
rainbow of blooms
waiting,
like open pots of paint,
for her artistry:
Elegant iris
in purple gowns
pink button carnations
flat-faced white daisies
peach tulips not yet
revealing the black stars within
delicate green ferns
bold tiger lilies
four varieties of rose.

As she selects stems for
a bridal bouquet
a birthday arrangement
and two funerals wreaths,
hope bursts
from the palms
of her hands.

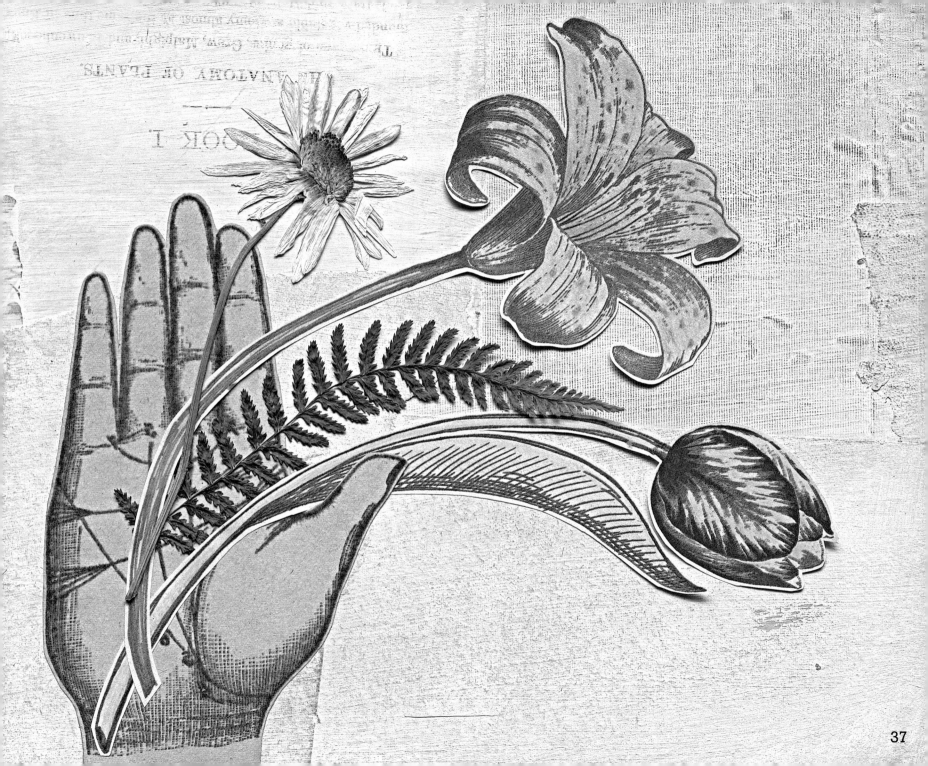

mail carrier

After twenty years of driving
the same route
six days a week,
the mail carrier
can tell you the name
of everyone on her ten-mile loop—
what magazines people read
who keeps a tidy lot
and where all the yappy dogs live.

She's a witness to a whole generation
of kids,
who went from tricycles
to first cars
as her white truck metered out days.

Entrepreneur

At seven
she created perfumes
by crushing blooms from her mother's
roses and lavender plants.

At fourteen
she concocted nail polishes
in shocking shades,
first selling to her friends
(just to replace ingredients),
then to boutique owners downtown.

Now she employs
four other teens
in her factory and warehouse
(a converted shed)
to fill orders,
experiment
with seasonal tints.

Next year she'll study business
at the community college,
paying the tuition
from profits
already earning interest
in a strong mutual fund.

FILMMAKER

For now,
the filmmaker
scoops popcorn
into cardboard buckets
pushes large sodas
and nacho combos
to young families
and couples out on
first dates.

Waiting
to sweep up messes
between the long rows of well-worn seats,
she watches the credits flicker and roll
on the silver screen
and dreams
that one day her name
will appear
first.

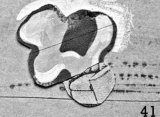

41

waiter

The waiter pings
between tables.
Table two needs
more water.
Table four wants ketchup.
At table six the toddler
tipped his milk.
More napkins—
quick!

The waiter zips over
wipes up the mess
fetches the ketchup
fills glasses with clacking cubes
of ice water
tops off two decaf coffees
delivers identical dinners
remembers to smile.

janitor

The janitor
knows
what's hidden behind
locked doors
lurking in dark corners
and tucked into closets.
He senses
all the secret wishes
a building whispers
in the night.

43

BABYSITTER

The babysitter
checks the bars on her cell,
drops it into the dark hole of her backpack
with loot for her charges:
a coloring book with only two pages used
a sheet of stickers
a movie about a rescue dog
and a handful of chocolates
for serious meltdowns,
boo-boos, or bribes.

She hops the fence
and surrenders
to tea parties
block castles
and books
that have long ago been memorized.

After getting the kids to sleep,
she calls her one-and-only true best friend
to dissect every thought from the
entire
four hours
since they last spoke—
till the sound of keys
startles the brass doorknob.

programmer

After ten hours
translating symbols and letters
(modern hieroglyphics)
on her computer screen,
the programmer
sees the code scroll
even when
she snaps her heavy lids
closed
over bloodshot eyes.

Ironic
that only
when she admits defeat,
collapsing onto her unmade bed
and descending
into a tangled maelstrom of dreams,
the golden key
to the glitch in the program
drops from
the tornado of images
and lands next to the blue glow
of her alarm clock.

camp counselor

After the campers
drift off to sleep
the counselor
slips out into
the cool, damp night
to meet new best friends.

They roll out sleeping bags
And—too tired to speak—
point out shooting stars
and listen to the
tink
tink
tink
of the flag hook against
the empty pole,
the restless crickets,
the bullfrog by the riverbank.
Then they slip into the arms of sleep,
never stirring
until the barred owl's haunting cry
wakes them
just before dawn.

NIGHT

As the sun
pulls pastel sheets over her head
the writer logs off
the babysitter yawns
the artist drops brushes into turpentine
the welder changes clothes
the waiter counts tips.
Keys jingle
lights snap off
cell phones blare.

Then the moon
unlocks the door
for the night shift.